"The Irish Twins"

by Lucy Fitch Perkins

Originally published in 1913.

Table of Contents:

Chapter One.

Grannie Malone and the Twins.

One day of the world, when it was young summer in
Ireland, old Grannie Malone sat by her fireplace knitting.
She was all alone, and in her lap lay a letter.

Sometimes she took the letter in her hands, and turned it
over and over, and looked at it. Then she would put it down
again with a little sigh.

"If I but had the learning," said Grannie Malone to herself,
"I could be reading Michael's letters without calling in the
Priest, and 'tis long since he passed this door. 'Tis hard
work waiting until some one can tell me what at all is in it."

She stooped over and put a bit of peat on the fire, and
because she had no one else to talk to, she talked to the tea-
kettle. "There now," she said to it, "'tis a lazy bit of steam
that's coming out of the nose of you! I'll be wanting my tea
soon, and no water boiling."

She lifted the lid and peeped into the kettle. "'Tis empty
entirely!" she cried, "and a thirsty kettle it is surely, and no
one but myself to fetch and carry for it!"

She got up slowly, laid her knitting and the letter on the
chair, took the kettle off the hook, and went to the door.

There was but one door and one window in the one little
room of her cabin, so if the sun had not been shining
brightly it would have been quite dark within.

But the upper half of the door stood open, and the afternoon sun slanted across the earthen floor and brightened the dishes that stood on the old dresser. It even showed Grannie Malone's bed in the far end of the room, and some of her clothes hanging from the rafters overhead.

There was little else in the room to see, except her chair, a wooden table, and a little bench by the fire, a pile of peat on the hearth, and a bag of potatoes in the corner. Grannie Malone opened the lower half of the door and stepped out into the sunshine. Some speckled hens that had been sunning themselves on the doorstep fluttered out of the way, and then ran after her to the well. "Shoo—get along with you!" cried Grannie Malone. She flapped her apron at them. "'Tis you that are always thinking of something to eat! Sure, there are bugs enough in Ireland, without your always being at my heels to be fed! Come now,—scratch for your living like honest hens, and I'll give you a sup of water if it's dry you are." The well had a stone curb around it, and a bucket with a rope tied to it stood on the curb. Grannie let the bucket down into the well until she heard it strike the fresh spring water with a splash. Then she pulled and pulled on the rope. The bucket came up slowly and water spilled over the sides as Grannie lifted it to the curb.

She poured some of the water into the dish for the hens, filled her kettle, and then straightened her bent back, and stood looking at the little cabin and the brown bog beyond.

"Sure, it's old we all are together," she said to herself, nodding her head. "The old cabin with the rain leaking through the thatch of a wet day, and the old well with moss on the stones of it. And the hens themselves, too old to cook, and too old to be laying,—except on the doorstep in the sunshine, the creatures!—But 'tis home, thanks be to God."

She lifted her kettle and went slowly back into the house. The hens followed her to the door, but she shut the lower half of it behind her and left them outside.

She went to the fireplace and hung the kettle on the hook, blew the coals to a blaze with a pair of leaky bellows, and sat down before the fire once more to wait for the water to boil.

She knit round and round her stocking, and there was no sound in the room but the click-click of her needles, and the tick-tick of the clock, and the little purring noise of the fire on the hearth.

Just as the kettle began to sing, there was a squawking among the hens on the doorstep, and two dark heads appeared above the closed half of the door.

A little girl's voice called out, "How are you at all, Grannie Malone?"

And a little boy's voice said, "We've come to bring you a sup of milk that Mother sent you."

Grannie Malone jumped out of her chair and ran to the door. "Och, if it's not the McQueen Twins—the two of them!" she cried. "Bless your sweet faces! Come in, Larry and Eileen! You are as welcome as the flowers of spring. And how is your Mother, the day? May God spare her to her comforts for long years to come!" She swung the door open as she talked, took the jug from Eileen's hand, and poured the milk into a jug of her own that stood on the dresser.

"Sure, Mother is well. And how is yourself, Grannie Malone?" Eileen answered, politely.

"Barring the rheumatism and the asthma, and the old age in my bones, I'm doing well, thanks be to God," said Grannie Malone. "Sit down by the fire, now, till I wet a cup of tea and make a cakeen for you! And indeed it's yourselves can read me a letter from my son Michael, that's in America! It has been in the house these three days waiting for some one with the learning to come along by."

She ran to the chair and picked up the letter. The Twins sat down on a little bench by the fireplace, and Grannie Malone put the letter in their hands.

"We've not got all the learning yet," Larry said. "We might not be able to read it."

"You can try," said Grannie Malone.

Then she opened the letter, and a bit of folded green paper with printing on it fell out. "God bless the boy," she cried, "there's one of those in every letter he sends me! 'Tis money that is! Can you make out the figures on it, now?"

Larry and Eileen looked it over carefully. "There it is, hiding in the corner," said Larry. He pointed to a "5" on the green paper.

"Five pounds it is!" said Grannie Malone. "Sure it's a fortune! Oh, it's himself is the good son to me! What does the letter say?"

The Twins spread the sheet open and studied it, while Grannie hovered over them, trembling with excitement.

"Sure, that's Dear, isn't it?" said Eileen, pointing to the first word.

"Sure," said Larry; "letters always begin like that."

"Dear G-r-a-n-n-i-e," spelt Eileen. "What could that be but Grannie?"

"'Tis from my grandson, young Patrick, then," cried Grannie. "Indeed, he's but the age of yourselves! How old are you at all?"

"We're seven," said the Twins.

"Patrick might be eight," said his Grandmother, "but surely the clever children like yourselves and the two of you together should be able to make it out. There's but one of Patrick, and there should be more learning between the two of you than in one alone, even though he is a bit older! Try now."

Larry and Eileen tried. This was the letter. It was written in a large staggery hand.

"Will you listen to that now!" cried Grannie Malone. "Is it taking me back to America, he'd be! 'Tis a terrible journey altogether, and a strange country at the end of it, for me to be laying my old bones in! But I'd be a proud woman to see my own son, in any country of the world, and he an alderman!"

There was a letter from Michael himself in the envelope also, but the Twins could not read that, however much they tried.

So Grannie was obliged to put the two letters and the green paper under the clock over the fireplace, to wait until the Priest should pass that way.

Chapter Two.

The Tea-Party.

"Sure, this is a fine day for me, altogether," said Grannie
Malone as she got out her bit of flour to make the cake. "I
can wait for the letter from himself, the way I know they're
in health, and have not forgotten their old Mother. Troth,
we'll have a bit of a feast over it now," she said to the
Twins. "While I'm throwing the cakeen together do you get
some potatoes from the bag, Eileen, and put them down in
the ashes, and you, Larry, stir up the fire a bit, and keep the
kettle full. Sure, 'tis singing away like a bird this instant
minute! Put some water in it, avic, and then shut up the
hens for me."

Eileen ran to the potato bag in the corner and took out four
good-sized potatoes. "There's but three of us," she said to
herself, "but Larry will surely be wanting two, himself."

She got down on her knees and buried the potatoes in the
burning peat. Then she took a little broom that stood near
by, and tidied up the hearth.

Larry took the kettle to the well for more water. He slopped
a good deal of it as he came back. It made great spots of
mud, for there was no wooden floor—only hard earth with
flat stones set in it.

"Arrah now, Larry, you do be slopping things up the equal
of a thunderstorm," Eileen said to him.

"Never you mind that, now, Larry," said Grannie Malone.
"It might have been that the kettle leaked itself, and no

fault of your own at all! Sure, a bit of water here or there does nobody any harm."

She hung the tea-kettle on the hook over the fire again. Then she brought the cakeen and put it into a small iron baking-kettle, and put a cover over it. She put turf on top of the cover. "'Twill not be long until it's baked," said Grannie, "and you can be watching it, Eileen, while I set out the table."

She pulled a little wooden table out before the fire, put three plates and three cups on it, some salt, and the jug of milk. Meanwhile Larry was out trying to shut the hens into the little shelter beside the house. But he couldn't get them all in. One old speckled hen ran round the house to the door. Larry ran after her. The hen flew up on top of the half-door. She was very much excited. "Cut-cut-cut," she squawked.

"Cut-cut yourself now!" cried Grannie Malone.

She ran toward the door, waving her spoon. "Shoo along out of this with your bad manners!" she cried.

Just that minute Larry came up behind the hen and tried to catch her by the legs.

"Cut-cut-cut-a-cut," squawked old Speckle; and up she flew, right over Grannie's head, into the rafters! Then she tucked herself cozily down to go to sleep.

"Did you ever see the likes of that old Speckle, now?" cried Grannie Malone. She ran for the broom. "Sure she must be after thinking I was lonesome for a bit of company! Do you think I'd be wanting you at all, you silly, when I have the

Twins by me?" she said to the hen. She shook the broom at her, but old Speckle wasn't a bit afraid of Grannie; she didn't move.

Then Grannie Malone put the broom under her and tried to lift her from her perch, but old Speckle had made up her mind to stay. So she flew across to another rafter, and lit on Grannie Malone's black coat that she wore to Mass on Sundays. She thought it a pleasant warm place and sat down again.

"Bad luck to you for an ill-favoured old thief!" screamed Grannie. "Get off my Sunday cloak with your muddy feet! It's ruined you'll have me entirely!"

She shook the cloak. Then old Speckle, squawking all the way, flew over to Grannie's bed! She ran the whole length of it. She left a little path clear across the patchwork quilt. Larry stood in one corner of the room waving his arms. Eileen was flapping her apron in another, while Grannie Malone chased old Speckle with the broom. At last, with a final squawk, she flew out of the door, and ran round to the shelter where the other hens were, and went in as if she thought home was the best place for a hen after all. Larry shut her in.

As soon as the hen was out of the house, Eileen screamed, "I smell something burning!"

"'Tis the cakeen," cried Grannie.

She and Eileen flew to the fireplace. Eileen got there first. She knocked the cover off the little kettle with the tongs, and out flew a cloud of smoke.

"Och, murder! 'Tis destroyed entirely!" poor Grannie groaned.

"I'll turn it quick," said Eileen.

She was in such a hurry she didn't wait for a fork or stick or anything! She took right hold of the little cakeen, and lifted it out of the kettle with her hand!

The little cake was hot! "Ow! Ow!" shrieked Eileen, and she dropped it right into the ashes! Then she danced up and down and sucked her fingers.

"The Saints help us! The cakeen is bewitched," wailed poor Grannie. She picked it up, and tossed it from one hand to the other, while she blew off the ashes.

Then she dropped it, burned side up, into the kettle once more, clapped on the cover, and set it where it would cook more slowly.

When that was done, she looked at Eileen's fingers. "It's not so bad at all, mavourneen, praise be to God," she said. "Sure, I thought I had you killed entirely, the way you screamed!"

"Eileen is always burning herself," said Larry. "Mother says 'tis only when she's burned up altogether that she'll learn to keep out of the fire at all!"

"'Twas all the fault of that disgraceful old hen," Grannie Malone said. "Sure, I'll have to be putting manners on her! She's no notion of behaviour at all, at all. Reach the sugar bowl, Larry, avic, and sit down by the table and rest your bones. I'll have the tea ready for you in a minute. Sit you

down, too, Eileen, while I get the potatoes." She took the
tongs and drew out the potatoes, blew off the ashes, and put
them on the table. Then she poured the boiling water over
the tea-leaves, and set the tea to draw, while she took the
cakeen from the kettle.

"'Tis not burned so much, after all," she said, as she looked
it over. "Sure, we can shut our eyes when we eat it."

She drew her own chair up to the table; the Twins sat on
the bench on the other side. Grannie Malone crossed
herself, and then they each took a potato, and broke it open.
They put salt on it, poured a little milk into the skin which
they held like a cup, and it was ready to eat.

Grannie poured the tea, and they had milk and sugar in it.
The little cakeen was broken open and buttered, and,
"Musha, 'tis fit for the Queen herself," said Larry, when he
had taken his first bite.

And Eileen said, "Indeed, ma'am, it's a grand cook you are
entirely."

"Sure, I'd need to be a grand cook with the grand company
I have," Grannie answered politely, "and with the fine son I
have in America to be sending me a fortune in every letter!
'Tis a great thing to have a good son, and do you be that
same to your Mother, the both of you, for 'tis but one
Mother that you'll get in all the world, and you've a right
to be choice of her."

"Sure, I'll never at all be a good son to my Mother,"
laughed Eileen.

"Well, then," said Grannie, "you can be a good daughter to her, and that's not far behind. Whist now, till I tell you the story of the Little Cakeen, and you'll see that 'tis a good thing entirely to behave yourselves and grow up fine and respectable, like the lad in the tale. It goes like this now:—"

"It was once long ago in old Ireland, there was living a fine, clean, honest, poor widow woman, and she having two sons (Note 1), and she fetched the both of them up fine and careful, but one of them turned out bad entirely. And one day she says to him, says she:—

"'I've given you your living as long as ever I can, and it's you must go out into the wide world and seek your fortune.'

"'Mother, I will,' says he.

"'And will you take a big cake with my curse, or a little cake with my blessing?' says she.

"'A big cake, sure,' says he.

"So she baked a big cake and cursed him, and he went away laughing! By and by, he came forninst a spring in the woods, and sat down to eat his dinner off the cake, and a small, little bird sat on the edge of the spring.

"'Give me a bit of your cake for my little ones in the nest,' said she; and he caught up a stone and threw at her.

"'I've scarce enough for myself,' says he, and she being a fairy, put her beak in the spring and turned it black as ink, and went away up in the trees. And whiles he looked for a stone for to kill her, a fox went away with his cake!

"So he went away from that place very mad, and next day he stopped, very hungry, at a farmer's house, and hired out for to tend the cows.

"'Be wise,' says the farmer's wife, 'for the next field is belonging to a giant, and if the cows get into the clover, he will kill you dead as a stone.'

"But the bad son laughed and went out to watch the cows; and before noontime he went to sleep up in the tree, and the cows all went in the clover. And out comes the giant and shook him down out of the tree and killed him dead, and that was the end of the bad son.

"And the next year the poor widow woman says to the good son:—

"'You must go out into the wide world and seek your fortune, for I can keep you no longer,' says the Mother.

"'Mother, I will,' says he.

"'And will you take a big cake with my curse or a little cake with my blessing?'

"'A little cake,' says he.

"So she baked it for him and gave him her blessing, and he went away, and she a-weeping after him fine and loud. And by and by he came to the same spring in the woods where the bad son was before him, and the small, little bird sat again on the side of it.

"'Give me a bit of your cakeen for my little ones in the nest,' says she.

"'I will,' says the good son, and he broke her off a fine piece, and she dipped her beak in the spring and turned it into sweet wine; and when he bit into his cake, sure, it was turned into fine plum-cake entirely; and he ate and drank and went on light-hearted. And next day he comes to the farmer's house.

"'Will ye tend the cows for me?' says the farmer.

"'I will,' says the good son.

"'Be wise,' says the farmer's wife, 'for the clover-field beyond is belonging to a giant, and if you leave in the cows, he will kill you dead.'

"'Never fear,' says the good son, 'I don't sleep at my work.'

"And he goes out in the field and lugs a big stone up in the tree, and then sends every cow far out in the clover-fields and goes back again to the tree! And out comes the giant a-roaring, so you could hear the roars of him a mile away, and when he finds the cow-boy, he goes under the tree to shake him down, but the good little son slips out the big stone, and it fell down and broke the giant's head entirely. So the good son went running away to the giant's house, and it being full to the eaves of gold and diamonds and splendid things.

"So you see what fine luck comes to folks that is good and honest! And he went home and fetched his old Mother, and they lived rich and contented, and died very old and respected."

"Do you suppose your son Michael killed any giants in America, the way he got to be an Alderman?" asked Eileen, when Grannie had finished her story.

"I don't rightly know that," Grannie answered. "Maybe it wasn't just exactly giants, but you can see for yourself that he is rich and respected, and he with a silk hat, and riding in a procession the same as the Lord-Mayor himself!"

"Did you ever see a giant or a fairy or any of the good little people themselves, Grannie Malone?" Larry asked.

"I've never exactly seen any of them with my own two eyes," she answered, "but many is the time I've talked with people and they having seen them. There was Mary O'Connor now,—dead long since, God rest her. She told me this tale herself, and she sitting by this very hearth. Wait now till I wet my mouth with a sup of tea in it, and I'll be telling you the tale the very same way she told it herself."

Note 1. Adapted from "Marygold House," in Play-Days, by Sarah Orne Jewett.

Chapter Three.

The Tale of the Leprechaun.

Grannie reached for the teapot and poured herself a cup of tea. As she sipped it, she said to the twins, "Did you ever hear of the Leprechauns? Little men they are, not half the bigness of the smallest baby you ever laid your two eyes on. Long beards they have, and little pointed caps on the heads of them.

"And it's forever making the little brogues (shoes) they are, and you can hear the tap-tap of their hammers before you ever get sight of them at all. And the gold and silver and precious things they have hidden away would fill the world with treasures.

"But they have the sharpness of the new moon, that's sharp at both ends, and no one can get their riches away from them at all. They do be saying that if you catch one in your two hands and never take your eyes off him, you can make him give up his money.

"But they've the tricks of the world to make you look the other way, the Leprechauns have. And then when you look back again, faith, they're nowhere at all!"

"Did Mary O'Connor catch one?" asked Eileen.

"Did she now!" cried Grannie. "Listen to this. One day Mary O'Connor was sitting in her bit of garden, with her knitting in her hand, and she was watching some bees that were going to swarm.

"It was a fine day in June, and the bees were humming, and the birds were chirping and hopping, and the butterflies were flying about, and everything smelt as sweet and fresh as if it was the first day of the world.

"Well, all of a sudden, what did she hear among the bean-rows in the garden but a noise that went tick-tack, tick-tack, just for all the world as if a brogue-maker was putting on the heel of a pump!

"'The Lord preserve us,' says Mary O'Connor; 'what in the world can that be?'

"So she laid down her knitting, and she went over to the beans. Now, never believe me, if she didn't see sitting right before her a bit of an old man, with a cocked hat on his head and a dudeen (pipe) in his mouth, smoking away! He had on a drab-coloured coat with big brass buttons on it, and a pair of silver buckles on his shoes, and he working away as hard as ever he could, heeling a little pair of pumps!

"You may believe me or not, Larry and Eileen McQueen, but the minute she clapped her eyes on him, she knew him for a Leprechaun.

"And she says to him very bold, 'God save you, honest man! That's hard work you're at this hot day!' And she made a run at him and caught him in her two hands!

"'And where is your purse of money?' says she.

"'Money!' says he; 'money is it! And where on top of earth would an old creature like myself get money?' says he.

"'Maybe not on top of earth at all, but in it,' says she; and with that she gave him a bit of a squeeze. 'Come, come,' says she. 'Don't be turning your tricks upon an honest woman!'

"And then she, being at the time as good-looking a young woman as you'd find, put a wicked face on her, and pulled a knife from her pocket, and says she, 'If you don't give me your purse this instant minute, or show me a pot of gold, I'll cut the nose off the face of you as soon as wink.'

"The little man's eyes were popping out of his head with fright, and says he, 'Come with me a couple of fields off, and I'll show you where I keep my money!'

"So she went, still holding him fast in her hand, and keeping her two eyes fixed on him without so much as a wink, when, all of a sudden, what do you think?

"She heard a whiz and a buzz behind her, as if all the bees in the world were humming, and the little old man cries out, 'There go your bees a-swarming and a-going off with themselves like blazes!'

"She turned her head for no more than a second of time, but when she looked back there was nothing at all in her hand.

"He slipped out of her fingers as if he were made of fog or smoke, and sorrow a bit of him did she ever see after." (Note 1.)

"And she never got the gold at all," sighed Eileen.

"Never so much as a ha'penny worth," said Grannie Malone.

"I believe I'd rather get rich in America than try to catch Leprechauns for a living," said Larry.

"And you never said a truer word," said Grannie. "'Tis a poor living you'd get from the Leprechauns, I'm thinking, rich as they are."

By this time the teapot was empty, and every crumb of the cakeen was gone, and as Larry had eaten two potatoes, just as Eileen thought he would, there was little left to clear away.

It was late in the afternoon. The room had grown darker, and Grannie Malone went to the little window and looked out.

"Now run along with yourselves home," she said, "for the sun is nearly setting across the bog, and your Mother will be looking for you. Here, put this in your pocket for luck." She gave Larry a little piece of coal. "The Good Little People will take care of good children if they have a bit o' this with them," she said; "and you, Eileen, be careful that you don't step in a fairy ring on your way home, for you've a light foot on you like a leaf in the wind, and 'The People' will keep you dancing for dear knows how long, if once they get you."

"We'll keep right in the boreen (road), won't we, Larry? Good-bye, Grannie," said Eileen.

The Twins started home. Grannie Malone stood in her doorway, shading her eyes with her hand, and looking after them until a turn in the road hid them from sight. Then she went into her little cabin and shut the door.

Note 1. Adapted from Thomas Keightley's Fairy Mythology.

Chapter Four.

The Tinkers.

After Larry and Eileen had gone around the turn in the road there were no houses in sight for quite a long distance.

On one side of the road stretched the brown bog, with here and there a pool of water in it which shone bright in the colours of the setting sun. It was gay, too, with patches of yellow buttercups, of primroses, and golden whins. The whins had been in bloom since Easter, for Larry and Eileen had gathered the yellow flowers to dye their Easter eggs. On the other side of the road the land rose a little, and was so covered with stones that it seemed as if there were no earth left for things to grow in. Yet the mountain fern took root there and made the rocks gay with its green fronds.

The sun was so low that their shadows stretched far across the bogland beside them as the Twins trudged along.

Three black ravens were flying overhead, and a lark was singing its evening song.

Eileen looked up in the sky. "There's the ghost of a moon up there! Look, Larry," she said.

Larry looked up. There floating high above them, was a pale, pale moon, almost the colour of the sky itself. "It looks queer and lonesome up there," he said, "and there's no luck at all in three ravens flying. They'll be putting a grudge on somebody's cow, maybe. I wonder where the little lark does be hiding herself."

Larry was still looking up in the sky for the little lark, when Eileen suddenly seized his arm. "Whist, Larry," she whispered. "Look before you on the road!"

Larry stopped stock-still and looked. A man was coming toward them. The man was still a long way off, but they could see that he carried something on his back. And beside the road, not so far away from where the Twins stood, there was a camp, like a gypsy camp.

"'Tis the Tinkers!" whispered Larry. He took Eileen's hand and pulled her with him behind a heap of stones by the road. Then they crept along very quietly and climbed over the wall into a field.

From behind the wall they could peep between the stones at the Tinkers' Camp without being seen.

The Twins were afraid of Tinkers. Everybody is in Ireland, because the Tinkers wander around over the country without having any homes anywhere.

They go from house to house in all the villages mending the pots and pans, and often they steal whatever they can lay their hands on.

At night they sleep on the ground with only straw for a bed, and they cook in a kettle over a camp-fire.

The Twins were so badly scared that their teeth chattered.

Eileen was the first to say anything.

"However will we g-g-g-get home at all?" she whispered.
"They've a dog with them, and he'll b-b-b-bark at us
surely. Maybe he'll bite us!"

They could see a woman moving about through the Camp.
She had a fire with a kettle hanging over it. There were two
or three other people about, and some starved-looking
horses. The dog was lying beside the fire, and there was a
baby rolling about on the ground. A little pig was tied by
one hind leg to a thorn-bush.

"If the dog comes after us," said Larry, "I'd drop a stone on
him, out of a tree, just the way the good son did in the
story, and kill him dead."

"But there's never a tree anywhere about," said Eileen.
"Sure, that is no plan at all."

"That's a true word," said Larry, when he had looked all
about for a tree, and found none. "We'll have to think of
something else."

Then he thought and thought. "We might go back to
Grannie's," he said after a while.

"That would be no better," Eileen whispered, "for, surely,
our Mother would go crazy with worrying if we didn't
come home, at all, and we already so late."

"Well, then," Larry answered, "we must just bide here until
it's dark, and creep by, the best way we can. Anyway, I've

the piece of coal in my pocket, and Grannie said no harm would come to us at all, and we having it."

Just then the man, who had been coming up the road, reached the Camp. The dog ran out to meet him, barking joyfully. The man came near the fire and threw the bundle off his shoulder. It was two fat geese, with their legs tied together!

"The Saints preserve us," whispered Eileen, "if those aren't our own two geese! Do you see those black feathers in their wings?"

"He's the thief of the world," said Larry.

He forgot to be frightened because he was so angry, and he spoke right out loud! He stood up and shook his fist at the Tinker. His head showed over the top of the wall. Eileen jerked him down.

"Whist now, Larry darling," she begged. "If the dog sees you once he'll tear you to pieces."

Larry dropped behind the wall again, and they watched the Tinker's wife loosen the string about the legs of the geese, and tie them by a long cord to the bush, beside the little pig. Then all the Tinker people gathered around the pot and began to eat their supper.

The baby and the dog were on the ground playing together. The Twins could hear the shouts of the baby, and the barks of the dog.

It was quite dusk by this time, but the moon grew brighter and brighter in the sky, and the flames of the Tinkers' fire glowed more and more red, as the night came on.

"Sure, it isn't going to get real dark at all," whispered Larry.

"Then we'd better be going now," said Eileen, "for the Tinkers are eating their supper, and their backs are towards the road, and we'll make hardly a taste of noise with our bare feet."

They crept along behind the rocks, and over the wall. "Now," whispered Larry, "slip along until we're right beside them, and then run like the wind!"

The Twins took hold of hands. They could hear their hearts beat. They walked softly up the road.

The Tinkers were still laughing and talking; the baby and the dog kept on playing.

The Twins were almost by, when all of a sudden, the geese stood up. "Squawk, squawk," they cried. "Squawk, squawk."

"Whatever is the matter with you, now?" said the Tinker's wife to the geese. "Can't you be quiet?" The dog stopped romping with the baby, sniffed the air, and growled. "Lie down," said the woman; "there's a bone for your supper." She threw the dog a bone. He sprang at it and began to gnaw it.

Larry and Eileen had crouched behind a rock the minute the geese began to squawk. "I believe they know us," whispered Eileen.

They waited until everything was quiet again. Then Larry whispered, "Run now, and if you fall, never wait to rise but run till we get to Tom Daly's house!"

Then they ran! The soft pat-pat of their bare feet on the dirt road was not heard by the Tinkers, and soon another turn in the road hid them from view, but, for all that, they ran and ran, ever so far, until some houses were in sight.

They could see the flicker of firelight in the windows of the nearest house. It was Tom Daly's house. They could see Tom's shadow as he sat at his loom, weaving flax into beautiful white linen cloth. They could hear the clack! clack! of his loom. It made the Twins feel much safer to hear this sound and see Tom's shadow, for Tom was a friend of theirs, and they often went into his house and watched him weave his beautiful linen, which was so fine that the Queen herself used it. Up the road, in the window of the last house of all, a candle shone.

"Sure, Mother is watching for us," said Larry. "She's put a candle in the window."

They went on more slowly now, past Tom Daly's, past the Maguires' and the O'Briens' and several other houses on the way, and when they were quite near their own home Larry said, "Sure, I'll never travel again without a bit of coal in my pocket. Look at all the danger we've been in this night, and never the smallest thing happening to us."

And Eileen said, "Indeed, musha, 'tis well we're the good children! Sure, the Good Little People would never at all let harm come to the likes of us, just as Grannie said."

Chapter Five.

The Twins get Home.

When they were nearly home, the Twins saw a dark figure hurrying down the road, and as it drew near, their Mother's voice called to them, "Is it yourselves, Larry and Eileen, and whatever kept you till this hour? Sure, you've had me distracted entirely with wondering what had become of you at all! And your Dada sits in the room with a lip on him as long as to-day and to-morrow!"

The Twins both began to talk at once. Their mother clapped her hands over her ears.

"Can't you hold your tongues and speak quietly now—one at a time like gentlemen and ladies?" she said. "Come in to your father and tell him all about it."

The Twins each took one of her hands, and they all three hurried into the house. They went into the kitchen. Their Father was sitting by the chimney, with his feet up, smoking his pipe when they came in. He brought his feet to the floor with a thump, and sat up straight in his chair.

"Where have you been, you Spalpeens?" he said. "It's nine o'clock this instant minute."

The Twins both began again to talk. Their Mother flew about the kitchen to get them a bite of supper.

"Come now," said the Father, "I can't hear myself at all with the noise of you. Do you tell the tale, Larry."

Then Larry told them about the cakeen, and the silk hat, and Michael Malone, and the Tinkers, while his Mother said, "The Saints preserve us!" every few words, and Eileen interrupted to tell how brave Larry had been—"just like the good son in Grannie Malone's tale, for all the world."

But when they came to the geese part of the story, the Father said, "Blathers," and got up and hurried out to the place where the fowls were kept, in the yard behind the house.

In a few minutes he came in again. "The geese are gone," he said, "and that's the truth or I can't speak it!"

"Bad luck to the thieves, then," cried the Mother. "The back of my hand to them! Sure, I saw a rough, scraggly man with a beard on him like a rick of hay, come along this very afternoon, and I up the road talking with Mrs Maguire! I never thought he'd make that bold, to carry off geese in the broad light of day! And me saving them against Christmastime, too!"

"Wait till I get that fellow where beating is cheap, and I'll take the change out of him!" said the Father.

Eileen began to cry and Larry's lip trembled.

"Come here now, you poor dears," their Mother said. "Sit down on the two creepeens by the fire, and have a bite to eat before you go to bed. Indeed, you must be starved entirely, with the running, and the fright, and all. I'll give you a drink of cold milk, warmed up with a sup of hot water through it, and a bit of bread, to comfort your stomachs."

While the Twins ate the bread and drank the milk, their Father and Mother talked about the Tinkers. "Sure, they are as a frost in spring, and a blight in harvest," said Mrs McQueen. "I wonder wherever they got the badness in them the way they have."

"I've heard said it was a Tinker that led Saint Patrick astray when he was in Ireland," said Mr McQueen. "I don't know if it's true or not, but the tale is that he was brought here a slave, and that it would take a hundred pounds to buy his freedom. One day, when he was minding the sheep on the hills, he found a lump of silver, and he met a Tinker and asked him the value of it.

"'Wirra,' says the Tinker, ''tis naught but a bit of solder. Give it to me!' But Saint Patrick took it to a smith instead, and the smith told him the truth about it, and Saint Patrick put a curse on the Tinkers, that every man's face should be against them, and that they should get no rest at all but to follow the road."

"Some say they do be walking the world forever," said Mrs McQueen, "and I never in my life met any one that had seen a Tinker's funeral."

"There'll maybe be one if I catch the Tinker that stole the geese!" Mr McQueen said grimly.

Mrs McQueen laughed. "It's the fierce one you are to talk," she said, "and you that good-natured when you're angry that you'd scare not even a fly! Come along now to bed with you," she added to the Twins. "There you sit with your eyes dropping out of your heads with sleep."

She helped them undress and popped them into their beds in the next room; then she barred the door, put out the candle, covered the coals in the fireplace, and went to bed in the room on the other side of the kitchen. Last of all, Mr McQueen knocked the ashes from his pipe against the chimney-piece, and soon everything was quiet in their cottage, and in the whole village of Ballymora where they lived.

Chapter Six.

How they went to the Bog.

The next morning when the Twins woke up, the sun was shining in through the one little square window in the bedroom, and lay in a bright patch of yellow on the floor. Eileen sat up in bed and rubbed her eyes. Then she stuck her head out between the curtains of her bed. "Is it to-day or to-morrow? I don't know," she said.

Larry sat up in his bed and rubbed his eyes. He peeped out from his curtains. "It isn't yesterday, anyway," he said, "and glad I am for that. Do you mind about the Tinkers, Eileen?"

"I do so," said Eileen, "and the geese."

Their Mother heard them and came to the door. "Sure, I thought I'd let you sleep as late as ever you liked," she said, "for there's no school to-day, but you're awake and clacking, so how would you like to go with your Dada to the bog to cut turf? Himself will put a bit of bread in his pocket for you, and you can take a sup of milk along."

"Oh, wirra!" cried Eileen. "What have we done but left the milk-jug at Grannie Malone's!"

"You can take the milk in the old brown jug, then," said the Mother, "and come along home by way of Grannie's, and get the jug itself. I'd like your Father to get a sight of the Tinkers' Camp, and maybe of that thief of the world that stole the geese on us."

It didn't take the Twins long to dress. They wore few clothes, and no shoes and stockings, and their breakfast of bread and potatoes was soon eaten. The Mother had already milked the cow, and when they had had a drink of fresh milk they were ready to start.

Mr McQueen was at the door with "Colleen," the donkey, and when Larry and Eileen came out, he put them both on Colleen's back, and they started down the road toward the bog.

When they came to the place where the Tinkers' Camp should be, there was no camp there at all! They looked east and west, but no sign of the Tinkers did they see.

"If it were not for the two geese gone, I'd think you had been dreaming!" said Mr McQueen to the Twins.

"Look there, then," said Larry. "Sure, there's the black mark on the ground where their fire was!"

The Twins slid off Colleen's back, and ran to the spot where the camp had been. There, indeed, was the mark of a fire, and near by were some wisps of straw. There were the marks of horses' feet, too, and Eileen found a white goose feather by the thorn-bush, and a piece of broken rope.

"They were here surely," Mr McQueen said, "and far enough away they are by this time, no doubt. It's likely the police were after them."

They went back to the road, and the Twins got up again on Colleen's back, and soon they had reached the near end of the bog.

Mr McQueen stopped. "I'll be cutting the turf here," he said, "and the two of you can go on to Grannie Malone's with the donkey, and bring back the jug with yourselves. Get along with you," and he gave the donkey a slap.

The Twins and the donkey started along the road. Everything went well until Colleen spied a tuft of green thistles, on a high bank beside the road. Colleen loved thistles, and she made straight for them. The first thing the Twins knew they were sliding swiftly down the donkey's back, while Colleen stood with her fore feet high on the bank and her hind feet in the road.

Larry, being behind, landed first, with Eileen on top of him. She wasn't hurt a bit, but she was a little scared. "Sure, Larry, but you're the soft one to fall on," she said as she rolled over and picked herself up.

"I may be soft to fall on," said Larry, "but I'm the easier squashed for that! Look at me now! It's out of shape I am entirely, with the print of yourself on me!"

Then—"Whatever will we do with Colleen?" Eileen said. "She's got her nose in the thistles and we'll never be able to drag her away from them."

They pulled on the halter, but Colleen refused to budge. Larry got up on the bank and pushed her. He even pulled her backward by the tail! Colleen didn't seem to mind it at all. She kept right on eating the thistles.

At last Larry said, "You go on with yourself to Grannie Malone's for the jug, Eileen, and I'll stay here until she finishes the thistles."

So he sat down by the road on a stone and Eileen trotted off to Grannie's.

Chapter Seven.

The Bog.

When Eileen got back with the jug, she found Larry still sitting beside the road. He was talking with a freckled-faced boy, and Colleen's head was still in the thistles.

"The top of the morning to you, Dennis Maguire," Eileen called to the freckled boy when she saw him. "And does it take the two of you to watch one donkey at his breakfast? Come along and let's play in the bog!"

"But however shall we leave Colleen? She might run away on us," said Larry.

"She's tethered by hunger fast enough," said Eileen. "Ropes would not drag her away. But you could throw her halter over a stone, to be sure."

Larry slipped the halter over a stone, they set the milk-jug in a safe place, and the three children ran off into the bog.

The bogland was brown and dark. Tufts of coarse grass grew here and there, and patches of yellow gorse. There were many puddles, and sometimes there were deep holes, where the turf had been cut out.

Mr McQueen was a thrifty man, and got his supply of turf early in the season. He would cut it out in long black blocks, like thick mud, and leave it in the sun to dry. When it was quite dry he would carry it home on Colleen's back, pile it in a high turf-stack near the kitchen door, and it would burn in the fireplace all winter.

The children were barefooted, so they played in the puddles as much as ever they liked.

By and by Eileen said, "Let's play we are Deirdre and the sons of Usnach."

"And who were they, indeed?" said Dennis.

"It was Grannie told us about them," said Eileen, "and sure it's the sorrowfullest story in Ireland."

"Then let's not be playing it," said Dennis.

"But there's Kings in it, and lots of fighting!"

"Well, then, it might not be so bad, at all. Tell the rest of it," Dennis answered.

"Well, then," Eileen began, "there once was a high King of Emain, and his name was Conchubar (pronounced Connor). And one time when he was hunting out in the fields, he heard a small little cry, crying. And he followed the sound of it, and what should he find, but a little baby girl, lying alone in the field!"

"Well, listen to that now," said Dennis.

"He did so," Eileen went on; "and he loved the child and took her to his castle, and had her brought up fine and careful, intending for to marry her when she should be grown up. And he hid her away, with only an old woman to take care of her, in a beautiful house far in the mountain, for he was afraid she'd be stolen away from him.

"And she had silver dishes and golden cups, and everything fine and elegant, and she the most beautiful creature you ever laid your two eyes on."

"Sure, I don't see much fighting in the tale, at all," said Dennis.

"Whist now, and I'll come to it," Eileen answered.

"One day when Deirdre had grown to be a fine big girl, she looks out of the window, and she sees Naisi (pronounced Naysha) going along by with his two brothers, the three of them together, they having been hunting in the mountain. And the minute she slaps her eyes on Naisi, 'There,' says she, 'is the grandest man in the width of the world, and I'll be wife to no man but him,' says she.

"So she calls in the sons of Usnach, though the old woman is scared to have her, and she tells Naisi she's going to marry him.

"And Naisi says, says he, 'I'll never be one to refuse a lady, but there'll be murder the day Conchubar finds it out!' says he.

"So they went away that same night, and the old woman fair distraught with fear. Soon along comes Conchubar to see Deirdre, for to marry her. And he had many men with him. When he finds Deirdre gone, 'It's that Naisi,' says he, 'that stole her away.' And he cursed him. And all his men and himself went out for to chase Naisi and his two brothers. But they never caught up with them at all for ten years, and Naisi and Deirdre living all the time as happy as two birds in the springtime."

"No fighting at all yet," said Dennis, "and ten years gone by. Musha, indeed, 'tis not much of a tale at all."

"There was fighting enough when the years were up," Eileen said. "The men of Conchubar pursued them up hill and down dale, and when they finally caught them, there was fighting that made the ground red with the blood spilled.

"And when Naisi and his brothers were all caught together, and Conchubar was after killing them, sure, didn't Deirdre put an end to herself entirely, and the four of them were buried together in one grave."

"But however will we play it at all?" said Larry.

"Listen, now," said Eileen. "I'll be Deirdre, of course. You can just be Naisi, Larry, and Dennis can be Conchubar, and he after us, and we running as fast as ever we can, to get away from him. You must give us a start, Dennis."

Chapter Eight.

"Diddy."

Larry and Eileen took hold of hands, and began running as fast as they could. They jumped from one tuft of grass to another. Dennis came splashing through the puddles after them. He had almost caught them, when all of a sudden, Larry stopped and listened.

"What's that now?" he said. Eileen and Dennis listened too. They heard a faint squealing sound.

They looked all around. There was nothing in sight but the brown bog, and the stones, and the blue hills far beyond. They were a little bit scared.

"Do you suppose it might be a Leprechaun?" Eileen whispered.

"'Tis a tapping noise they make; not a crying noise at all," Larry answered.

"Maybe it's a Banshee," Dennis said. "They do be crying about sometimes before somebody is going to die."

"'Tis no Banshee whatever," Eileen declared. "They only cry at night."

They heard the squealing sound again.

"'Tis right over there," cried Eileen, pointing to a black hole in the bog where turf had been cut out. "Indeed, and it might be a beautiful baby like Deirdre herself! Let's go and see."

They crept up to the bog-hole, and peeped over the edge. The hole was quite deep and down in the bottom of it was a little pig! Dennis rolled over on the ground beside the bog-hole and screamed with laughter.

"Sure, 'tis the beautiful child entirely!" he said.

"'Tis the little pig the Tinkers had!" cried Eileen.

"It broke the rope and ran away with itself," shouted Larry.

"However will we get it out?" said Eileen. "The hole is too deep entirely!"

"The poor little thing is nearly destroyed with hunger," Larry said. "I'll go down in the hole and lift her out."

"However will you get out yourself, then, Larry darling?" cried Eileen.

"The two of you can give me your hands," said Larry, "and I'll be up in no time."

Then Larry jumped down into the hole. He caught the little pig in his arms. The little pig squealed harder than ever and tried to get away, but Larry held it up as high as he could.

Eileen and Dennis reached down and each got hold of one of the pig's front feet. "Now then for you!" cried Larry.

He gave the pig a great shove. He shoved so hard that Eileen and Dennis both fell over backwards into a puddle!

But they held tight to the pig, and there the three of them were together, rolling in the bog with the pig on top of them!

"Hold her, hold her!" shrieked Larry. By standing on tiptoe his nose was just above the edge of the bog-hole, so he could see them.

"I've got her," Eileen cried. "Run back for the bit of rope the Tinkers left, Dennis, and tie her, hard and fast!"

Dennis ran for the rope while Eileen sat on the ground and held the little pig in her arms. The little pig squealed and kicked and tried every minute to get away. She kicked even after her hind legs were tied together. But Eileen held on!

"You'll have to get Larry out alone, Dennis, while I never let go of this pig," cried Eileen, breathlessly. "She's that wild, she'll be running away with herself on her two front legs, alone."

Dennis reached down, and took both of Larry's hands and pulled and pulled until he got him out.

Larry was covered with mud from the bog-hole, and Eileen and Dennis were wet and muddy from falling into the puddle.

But they had the pig!

"Sure, she is a beautiful little pig, and we'll call her Deirdre, because we found her in the bog just in the same way as Conchubar himself," said Larry.

"Indeed, Deirdre was too beautiful altogether to be naming a pig after her," Eileen said.

"Isn't she a beautiful little pig, then?" Larry answered.

"Well, maybe we might be calling her 'Diddy,' for short, and no offence to herself at all," Eileen agreed.

The poor little pig was so tired out with struggling, and so hungry, that she was fairly quiet while Dennis carried her on his shoulder to the road. Eileen walked behind Dennis and fed her with green leaves.

She was so quiet that Larry said: "We'll tie the rope to one of Diddy's hind legs, and she'll run home herself in front of us."

So when they reached the road he and Dennis tied the rope securely to Diddy's left hind leg and set her down.

They found Colleen asleep, standing up.

Larry woke her. Then he said, "Eileen, come now, you take the jug, and get on Colleen's back. Dennis can lead her, and I'll drive the pig myself."

But Diddy was feeling better after her rest. She made up her mind she didn't like the plan. She squealed and tried to get away. Once she turned quickly and ran between Larry's legs and tripped him up. But she was a tired little pig, and so it was not long before, somehow, they got her back to where Mr McQueen was working.

He hadn't heard them coming, though what with the pig squealing, and the children all speaking at once, they made noise enough. But Mr McQueen had his head down digging, and he was in a bog-hole besides, so when they came up right beside him, with the pig, he almost fell over with astonishment.

He stopped his work and leaned on his clete, while they told him all about the pig, and how they found it, and got it out of the hole, and how the Tinkers must have lost it. And when they were all done, he only said, "The Saints preserve us! We'll take it home to Herself and let her cosset it up a bit!"

So the children hurried off to take the pig to their Mother without even stopping to eat their bit of lunch. Mr McQueen came, too.

When they got home, they found Mrs McQueen leaning on the farmyard fence. When she saw them coming with the pig, she ran out to meet them.

"Wherever did you find the fine little pig?" she cried. Then she threw up her hands. "Look at the mud on you!" she said.

Then the Twins and Dennis told the story all over again, and Mrs McQueen took the little pig in her apron. "The poor little thing!" she said. "Its heart is beating that hard, you'd think its ribs would burst themselves. I'll get it some milk right away this minute when once you've looked in the yard."

Mr McQueen and Dennis and the Twins went to the fence. There in the yard were the two geese with the black feathers in their wings! "Faith, and the luck is all with us this day," said Mr McQueen. "However did you get them back at all?"

"'Twas this way, if you'll believe me," said Mrs McQueen. She scratched the little pig's back with one hand as she talked. "I was just after churning my butter when what should I see looking in the door but that thief of a Tinker with the beard like a rick of hay! Thinks I to myself, sure, my butter will be bewitched and never come at all with the bad luck of a stranger, and he a Tinker, coming in the house!

"But he comes in and gives one plunge to the dasher for luck and to break the spell, and says he, very civil, 'Would you be wanting to buy any fine geese to-day?'

"My heart was going thumpity-thump, but I says to him, 'I might look at them, maybe,' and with that I go to the door, for the sake of getting him out of it, and if there weren't our own two geese, with the legs of them tied together!"

"The impudence of that!" cried Mr McQueen. "Get along with your tale, woman! Surely you never paid the old thief for your own two geese!"

"Trust me!" replied Mrs McQueen. "I'm coming around to the point of my tale gradual, like an old goat grazing around its tethering stump! I says to him, 'They look well enough, but I'm wishful to see them standing up on their own two legs. That one looks as if it might be a bit lame, and the cord so tight on it! And meanwhile, will you be having a bit of a drink on this hot day?'

"Then I gave him a sup of milk, in a mug, and with that he thanks me kindly, loosens the cord, and sets the geese up on their legs for me to see. In a minute of time I stood between him and the geese, and 'Shoo!' says I to them, and to him I says, 'Get along with you before I call the man working behind the house to put an end to your thieving entirely!'

"And upon that he went in great haste, taking the mug along with him, but it was cracked anyway!"

"Woman, woman, but you've the clever tongue in your head," said Mr McQueen with admiration.

"'Tis mighty lucky we have," said Mrs McQueen, "for it's little else women have in this world to help themselves with!"

Then she put the little pig down in the empty pig-pen in the farmyard and went to fetch it some milk.

Chapter Nine.

The Secret.

Mr McQueen was a good farmer, but at the time he lived in Ireland, farmers could not own their farms.

The land was all owned by rich landlords, who did not do any work themselves. These landlords very often lived away in England or France, and did not know much about how the poor people lived at home, or how hard they had to work to get the money for the rent of their farms.

Sometimes, when they did know, they didn't care. What they wanted was all the money they could get, so they could live in fine houses and wear beautiful clothes, and go where they pleased, without doing any work.

When the landlords were away, they had agents to collect the rents for them.

The business of these agents was to get all the rent money they could, and they made life very hard for the farmers.

Sometimes when the farmers couldn't pay all the rent, the agent would turn them out of their houses. This was called "evicting" them. The farm that Mr McQueen lived on, as well as the village and all the country roundabout, was owned by the Earl of Elsmore, who lived most of the year in great style in England. The agent who collected rents was Mr Conroy. Nobody liked Mr Conroy very much, but everybody was afraid of him, because he could do so much to injure them.

So one morning when Mr McQueen came back very early from his potato-field, he was not glad to see Mr Conroy's horse standing near his door, and Mr Conroy himself, leaning on the farmyard fence, looking at the fowls.

"How are you, McQueen?" said Mr Conroy, when Mr McQueen came up.

"Well enough, Mr Conroy," said Mr McQueen.

"And you're doing well with the farm, too, it seems," said Mr Conroy. "Those are good-looking fowls you have, and the pig is fine and fat. How many cows have you, now?"

"Two, and a heifer," said Mr McQueen.

"You drained that field over by the bog this year, didn't you, and have it planted to turnips?" went on Mr Conroy. "I'm glad to see you so prosperous, McQueen. Of course, now, the farm is worth more than it was when you first took it, and so you'll not be surprised that I'm raising the rent on you."

"If the farm is worth more, 'tis my work that has made it so," said Mr McQueen, "and I shouldn't be punished for that. The house is none too good at all, and the place is not worth more. Last year was the drought and all manner of bad luck, and next year may be no better. Truly, Mr Conroy, if you press me, I don't know how I can scrape more together than I'm paying now."

"Well, then," said Mr Conroy. "You must just find a way, for this is one of the best farms about here, and you should pay as much as any one."

"You can't get money by shaking a man with empty pockets," said Mr McQueen.

But Mr Conroy only laughed and said:

"You'll have five pounds in yours when next rent-day comes around, or 'twill be the worse for you. You wouldn't like to be evicted, I'm sure."

Then he mounted his horse and rode away.

Mr McQueen went into the house with a heavy heart, and told his wife the bad news.

"Faith," said Mrs McQueen, "I'd not be in that man's shoes for all you could offer. It's grinding down the faces of the poor he is, and that at the telling of some one else! Not even his badness is his own! He does as he's bid."

"He gets fat on it," said Mr McQueen.

"Faith, we'll get along somehow," said Mrs McQueen. "We always have, though 'tis true it's been scant fare we've had now and again."

Mr McQueen didn't answer. He went back to his work in the fields. Mrs McQueen got the Twins started off to school, with their lunch in a little tin bucket, and began her washing, but she did not sing at her work that day as she sometimes did.

Larry and Eileen knew that something was wrong, though their Father and Mother had not said anything to them about it.

They had seen Mr Conroy talking with their Father in the yard. "And it's never a sign of anything good to see Mr Conroy," Eileen said.

Larry was thinking the same thing, for he said:—

"When I'm a man, I'm going to be rich, and then I'll give you and Mother and Dada a fine house, and fine clothes, and things in plenty."

"However will you get the money?" asked Eileen.

"Oh! Giants or something," Larry answered, "or maybe being an Alderman."

"Blathers!" said Eileen. "I've a better plan in my head. You know Dada and Mother said we could have Diddy for our very own, because we found her ourselves."

"I do," said Larry.

"Well, then," said Eileen, "I know it's about the rent they are bothered, for it always is the rent that bothers them. Now, when the Fair-time comes we'll coax Dada to let us take Diddy to the Fair. She'll be nice and fat by that time, and we'll sell her, and give the money to Dada for the rent!"

"Sure, it will be hard parting with Diddy, that's been like one of our own family since the day we found her crying in the bog," said Larry.

"Indeed, and it will," said Eileen, "but we think more of our parents than of a pig, surely."

"But however will we get her to the Fair to sell her?" said Larry.

"We'll get Dada to take her for us, but we'll never tell him we mean the money to go for the rent until we put it in his hands," Eileen answered, "and we won't tell any one else at all. It's a Secret."

"I'd like to be telling Dennis, maybe," said Larry.

"We can tell Dennis and Grannie Malone, but no one else at all," Eileen agreed.

Chapter Ten.

School.

By this time they had reached the schoolhouse. The Schoolmaster was standing in the door calling the children to come in.

He was a tall man dressed in a worn suit of black. He wore glasses on his nose, and carried a stick in his hand.

The schoolhouse had only one room, with four small windows, and Larry hung his cap and Eileen her shawl, on nails driven into the wall.

The schoolroom had benches for the children to sit on, with long desks in front of them. On the wall hung a printed copy of the Ten Commandments. At one side there was a fireplace, but, as it was summer, there was no fire in it.

The Master rapped on his desk, which was in the front of the room, and the children all hurried to their seats. Larry sat on one side of the room, with the boys. Eileen sat on the other, with the girls.

The Master called the roll. There were fifteen boys and thirteen girls. When the roll was called and the number marked down on a slate in front of the school, the Master said, "First class in reading."

All the little boys and girls of the size of Larry and Eileen came forward and stood in a row. There were just three of them: Larry and Eileen and Dennis.

"Larry, you may begin," said the Master.

Larry read the first lines of the lesson. They were, "To do ill is a sin.

"Can you run far?"

Larry wondered who it was that had done ill, and if he were running away because of it, and who stopped him to ask, "Can you run far?" He was thinking about it when Eileen read the next two sentences.

They were, "Is he friend or foe?

"Did you hurt your toe?"

This did not seem to Larry to clear the mystery.

"Next!" called the Master.

Dennis stood next. He read, "He was born in a house on the hill.

"Is rice a kind of corn?

"Get me a cork for the ink jar."

Just at this point the Master went to the open door to drive away some chickens that wanted to come in, and as Dennis had not been told to stop he went right on. Dennis was eight, and he could read quite fast if he kept his finger on the place. This is what he read:—

"The morn is the first part of the day.

"This is my son, I hope you will like him.

"Sin not, for God hates sin.

"Can a worm walk?

"No, it has no feet, but it can creep.

"Did you meet Fred in the street?

"Weep no more."

By this time the chickens were frightened away and Dennis was nearly out of breath.

The Master came back. Then Eileen had a turn. They could almost say the lessons by heart, they knew them so well.

After the reading-lesson they went back to their benches, and studied in loud whispers, but Larry was thinking of something else. He drew a pig with a curly tail on his slate—like this—

He held it up for Dennis to see. He wanted to tell him about Diddy and the Fair, but the Master saw what he had done. "Come here, Larry McQueen, and bring your slate," he said. "Sure, I'll teach you better manners. Get up on this stool now, and show yourself." He put a large paper dunce-cap on Larry's head, and made him sit up on a stool before the whole school!

The other children laughed, all but Eileen. She hid her face on her desk, and two little tears squeezed out between her fingers. But Larry didn't cry. He pretended he didn't care at all. He sat there for what seemed a very long time, while other children recited other lessons in reading, and grammar, and arithmetic. The Master gave him this poem to learn by heart:—

"I thank the Goodness and the Grace

That on my birth have smiled,

And made me in these Christian days,

A happy English child."

Larry wondered why he was called an English child, when he knew he was Irish. And he wasn't so sure either about the "Christian days"; but he learned it and said it to the teacher before he got down off the stool. It seemed to him that it was about three days before noontime came. At last they were dismissed, and the Twins went out with the other children into the schoolyard to eat their luncheon. Dennis ate his with them, and Larry told him the Secret.

After lunch they went back into the dark, smoky little schoolroom for more lessons, and when three o'clock came, how glad they were to go dancing out into the sunshine again, and walk home along the familiar road, with the air sweet about them, and the little birds singing in the fields.

Chapter Eleven.

The Fair.

For many weeks Eileen and Larry kept the Secret. They told no one but Dennis and Grannie Malone, and they both promised they would never, never tell.

Mr McQueen worked hard—early and late—over his turnips and cabbages and potatoes, and Larry and Eileen helped by feeding the pig and chickens, and driving the cows along the roadsides, where they could get fresh sweet grass to eat.

One evening Mr McQueen said to his wife. "Rent-day comes soon, and next week will be the Fair."

Larry and Eileen heard him say it. They looked at each other and then Eileen went to her Father and said, "Dada, will you take Larry and me to the Fair with you? We want to sell our pig."

"You sell your pig!" cried Mr McQueen. "You mean you want to sell it yourselves?"

"You can help us," Eileen answered; "but it's our pig and we want to sell it, don't we, Larry?"

Larry nodded his head up and down very hard with his mouth tight shut. He was so afraid the Secret would jump out of it!

"Well, I never heard the likes of that!" said McQueen. He slapped his knee and laughed.

"We've got it all planned," said Eileen. She was almost ready to cry because her Father laughed at her. "We've fed the pig and fed her, until she's so fat she can hardly walk, and we are going to wash her clean, and I have a ribbon to tie on her ear. Diddy will look so fine and stylish, I'm sure some one will want to buy her!"

Mrs McQueen was just setting away a pan of milk. She stopped with the pan in her hand.

"Leave them go," she said.

Mr McQueen smoked awhile in silence. At last he said:—

"It's your own pig, and I suppose you can go, but you'll have a long day of it."

"The longer the better," said the Twins.

All that week they carried acorns, and turnip-tops, and everything they could find that was good for pigs to eat, and fed them to Diddy, and she got fatter than ever.

The day before the Fair, they took the scrubbing-pail and the broom, and some water, and scrubbed her until she was all pink and clean. Then they put her in a clean place for the night, and went to bed early so they would be ready to get up in the morning.

When the first cock crowed, before daylight the next morning, Eileen's eyes popped wide open in the dark. The cock crowed again. Cock-a-doodle-doo!

"Wake up, Larry darling," cried Eileen from her bed. "The morn is upon us, and we are not ready for the Fair."

Larry bounded out of bed, and such a scurrying around as there was to get ready! Mrs McQueen was already blowing the fire on the hearth in the kitchen into a blaze, and the kettle was on to boil. The Twins wet their hair and their Mother parted it and then they combed it down tight on the sides of their heads. But no matter how much they wet their hair, the wind always blew it about their ears again in a very little while. They put on their best clothes, and then they were ready for breakfast.

Mr McQueen was up long before the Twins. He had harnessed Colleen and had loaded the pig into the cart somehow, and tied her securely. This must have been hard work, for Diddy had made up her mind she wasn't going to the Fair.

Mr McQueen had found room, too, for some crocks of butter, and several dozen eggs carefully packed in straw.

When breakfast was over, Mrs McQueen brought a stick with notches cut in it and gave it to Mr McQueen.

She explained what each notch meant. "There's one notch, and a big one, for selling the pig," she said, "and mind you see that the Twins get a good price for the creature. And here's another for selling the butter and eggs. And this is a pound of tea for Grannie Malone. She's been out of tea this week past, and she with no one to send. And this notch is for Mrs Maguire's side of bacon that you're to be after bringing her with her egg money, which is wrapped in a piece of paper in your inside pocket, and by the same token don't you be losing it.

"And for myself, there's so many things I'm needing, that I've put all these small notches close together. There's yarn for stockings for the Twins, and some thread for myself, to make crochet, that might turn me a penny in my odd moments, and a bit of flour, and some yellow meal. Now remember that you forget nothing of it all!" Mr McQueen shook his head sadly. "Faith, there's little pleasure in going to the Fair with so many things on my mind," he said.

The sun was just peeping over the distant hills, when Colleen started up the road, pulling the cart with Diddy in it, squealing "like a dozen of herself" Mrs McQueen said. Mr McQueen led the donkey, and Larry and Eileen followed on foot. They had on shoes and stockings, and Eileen had on a clean apron and a bright little shawl, so they looked quite gay.

They walked miles and miles, beside bogs, and over hills, along country roads bordered by hedgerows or by stone walls. At last they saw the towers of the Castle which belonged to the Earl of Elsmore. It was on top of a high hill.

The towers stood up strong and proud against the sky. Smoke was coming out of the chimneys.

"Do you suppose the Earl himself is at home?" Eileen asked her Father.

"'Tis not unlikely," Mr McQueen answered. "He comes home sometimes with parties of gentlemen and ladies for a bit of shooting or fishing."

"Maybe he'll come to the Fair," Eileen said to Larry.

"Sure, he'd never miss anything so grand as the Fair and he being in this part of the world," said Larry.

Some distance from the Castle they could see a church spire, and the roofs of the town, and nearer they saw a little village of stalls standing in the green field, like mushrooms that had sprung up overnight.

"The Fair! The Fair!" cried the Twins.

Chapter Twelve.

How they sold the Pig.

Although they had come so far, they were among the earliest at the Fair. People were hurrying to and fro, carrying all sorts of goods and arranging them for sale on counters in little stalls, around an open square in the centre of the grounds.

Cattle were being driven to their pens, horses were being brushed and curried, sheep were bleating, cows were lowing, and even the hens and ducks added their noise to the concert. Diddy herself squealed with all her might.

Larry and Eileen had never seen so many people together before in all their lives.

They had to think very hard about the Secret in order not to forget everything but the beautiful things they saw in the different stalls.

There were vegetables and meats, and butter and eggs. There were hats and caps. There were crochet-work, and bed-quilts, and shawls with bright borders, spread out for people to see.

There were hawkers going about with trays of things to eat, pies and sweets, toffee and sugar-sticks. This made the Twins remember that they were dreadfully hungry after their long walk, but they didn't have anything to eat until quite a while after that, because they had so much else to do. They followed their Father to the corner where the pigs were. A man came to tell them where to put Diddy.

"You can talk with these two farmers," said Mr McQueen.
He brought the Twins forward. "It's their pig."

Then Larry and Eileen told the man about finding Diddy in
the bog, and that their Father had said they could have her
for their own, and so they had come to the Fair to sell her.

"And whatever will you do with all the money?" asked the
man.

The Twins almost told! The Secret was right on the tip end
of their tongues, but they clapped their hands over their
mouths, quickly, so it didn't get out.

The man laughed. "Anyway, it's a fine pig, and you've a
right to get a good price for her," he said. And he gave
them the very best pen of all for Diddy.

When she was safely in the pen, Eileen and Larry tied the
red ribbon, which Eileen had brought in her pocket, to
Diddy's ear, and another to her tail. Diddy looked very gay.

When the Twins had had a bite to eat, they stood up before
Diddy's pen, where the man told them to, and Diddy stood
up on her hind legs with her front feet on the rail, and
squealed. Larry and Eileen fed her with turnip-tops.

There were a great many people in the Fairgrounds by that
time. They were laughing and talking, and looking at the
things in the different booths. Every single one of them
stopped to look at Diddy and the Twins, because the Twins
were the very youngest farmers in the whole Fair.

Everybody was interested, but nobody offered to buy, and
the Twins were getting discouraged when along came some

farmers with ribbons in their hands. They were the Judges!

The Twins almost held their breath while the Judges looked Diddy over. Then the head man said, "That's a very fine pig, and young. She is a thoroughbred. Wherever did you get her, Mr McQueen?"

Mr McQueen just said, "Ask them!" pointing to the Twins.

The Twins were very much scared to be talking to the Judges, but they told about the Tinkers and how they found Diddy in the bog, and the Judges nodded their heads and looked very wise, and finally the chief one said, "Faith, there's not her equal in the whole Fair! She gets the blue ribbon, or I'm no Judge."

All the other men said the same. Then they gave the blue ribbon to the Twins, and Eileen tied it on Diddy's other ear! Diddy did not seem to like being dressed up. She wiggled her ears and squealed.

Just then there was the gay sound of a horn. Tara, tara, tara! it sang, and right into the middle of the Fairground drove a great tally-ho coach, with pretty young ladies and fine young gentlemen riding on top of it.

Everybody turned away from Diddy and the Twins to see this grand sight!

The footman jumped down and helped down the ladies, while the driver, in livery, stood beside the horses' heads with his hand on their bridles.

Then all the young gentlemen and ladies went about the Fair to see the sights.

"'Tis a grand party from the Castle," said Mr McQueen to
the Twins. "And sure, that's the Earl's daughter, the Lady
Kathleen herself, with the pink roses on her hat! I haven't
seen a sight of her since she was a slip of a girl, the size of
yourselves."

Lady Kathleen and her party came by just at that moment,
and when she saw Diddy with her ribbons and the Twins
beside her, the Lady Kathleen stopped.

The Twins could hardly take their eyes off her sweet face
and her pretty dress, and the flowered hat, but she asked
them all sorts of questions, and finally they found
themselves telling her the story of how they found the pig.

"And what is your pig's name?" said Lady Kathleen.

"Sure, ma'am, it's Deirdre, but we call her Diddy for
short," Eileen answered.

All the young gentlemen and ladies laughed. The Twins
didn't like to be laughed at—they were almost ready to cry.

"And why did you call her Deirdre?" asked Lady Kathleen.

"It was because of finding her in the bog all alone with
herself, the same as Deirdre when she was a baby and
found by the high King of Emain," Eileen explained.

"A very good reason, and it's the finest story in Ireland,"
said Lady Kathleen. "I'm glad you know it so well, and she
is such a fine pig that I'm going to buy her from you
myself."

All the young ladies seemed to think this very funny, indeed. But Lady Kathleen didn't laugh. She called one of the footmen. He came running. "Do you see that this pig is sent to the Castle when the Fair is over," she said.

"I will, your Ladyship," said the footman. Then Lady Kathleen took out her purse. "What is the price of your pig?" she said to the Twins.

They didn't know what to say, but the Judge, who was standing near, said, "She is a high-bred pig, your Ladyship, and worth all of three pounds."

"Three pounds it is, then," said the Lady Kathleen. She opened her purse and took out three golden sovereigns.

She gave them to the Twins and then almost before they found breath to say, "Thank you, ma'am," she and her gay company had gone on to another part of the Fair. The Judge made a mark on Diddy's back to show that she had been sold.

The Twins gave the three golden sovereigns to their Father to carry for them, and he put them in the most inside pocket he had, for safe keeping! Then while he stayed to sell his butter and eggs, and to do his buying, the Twins started out to see the Fair by themselves.

Chapter Thirteen.

What they saw.

The first person they stopped to watch was a Juggler doing tricks. It was quite wonderful to see him keep three balls in the air all at the same time, or balance a pole on the end of his nose. But when he took out a frying-pan from behind his stall, and said to the Twins, who were standing right in front of him, "Now, I'll be after making you a bit of an omelet without any cooking," their eyes were fairly popping out of their heads with surprise.

The Juggler broke an egg into the frying-pan. Then he clapped on the cover, waved the pan in the air, and lifted the cover again. Instead of an omelet there in the frying-pan was a little black chicken crying "Peep, peep," as if it wanted its mother!

The Juggler looked very much surprised himself, and the Twins were simply astonished.

"Will you see that now!" Larry whispered to Eileen. "Sure, if only Old Speckle could be learning that trick, 'twould save her a deal of sitting."

"Indeed, then, 'tis magic," Eileen answered back, "and there's no luck in that same! Do you come away now, Larry McQueen, or he might be casting his spells on yourself and turning you into something else entirely, a goat maybe, or a Leprechaun!"

This seemed quite likely to Larry, too, so they slipped hurriedly out under the elbows of the crowd just as the

Juggler was in the very act of finding a white rabbit in the crown of his hat. They never stopped running until they found themselves in the middle of a group of people in a distant part of the Fairgrounds.

This crowd had gathered around a rough-looking man with a bundle of papers under his arm. He was waving a leaflet in the air and shouting, "Ladies and Gentlemen—Whist now till I sing you a song of Old Ireland. 'Tis the Ballad of the Census Taker!" Then he began to sing in a voice as loud as a clap of thunder. This was the first verse of the song:—

"Oh, they're taking of the Census

In the country and the town.

Have your children got the measles?

Are your chimneys tumbling down?"

Every one seemed to think this a very funny song and at the end of the second verse they all joined in the chorus. The Ballad Singer sang louder than all the rest of the people put together.

"Musha, the roars of him are like the roars of a giant," Eileen said to Larry. "Indeed, I'm fearing he'll burst himself with the noise that's in him."

The moment the song ended, the Ballad Singer passed the hat, and the crowd began to melt away. "There you go, now," cried the Singer, "lepping away on your two hind legs like scared rabbits! Come along back now, and buy the

Ballad of 'The Peeler and the Goat.' Sure, 'tis a fine song entirely and one you'll all be wanting to sing yourselves when once you've heard it." He seized a young man by the arm. "Walk up and buy a ballad now," he said to him. "Troth, you've the look of a fine singer yourself, and dear knows what minute you may be needing one, and none handy. Come now, buy before 'tis too late."

The young man turned very red. "I don't think I'll be wanting any ballads," he said, and tried to pull away.

"You don't think!" shouted the Ballad Singer. "Of course, you don't think, you've nothing whatever to do it with!"

The crowd laughed. The poor young man bought a ballad.

"There now," cried the Singer, "you're the broth of a boy after all! Who'll be after buying the next one off of me?"

His eyes lighted on the Twins. They shook in their shoes. "He'll be clapping one of them on us next," Larry said to Eileen. "We'd best be going along;" and they crept out of the crowd just as he began to roar out a new song.

An old woman, with a white cap and a shawl over her head and a basket on her arm, smiled at them as they slipped by. She jerked her thumb over her shoulder at the Ballad Singer. "Melodious is the closed mouth," she said.

"Indeed, ma'am, I've often heard my Mother say so," Eileen answered politely. She curtsied to the old woman.

The old woman looked pleased. "Will you come along with me out of the sound of this—the both of you?" she said. "And I'll take you to hear things that will keep the memory of Ireland green while there's an Irishman left in the world."

She led them to a raised platform some distance away. Over the platform there floated a white flag with a green harp on it. The old woman pointed to it. "Do you remember the old harp of Tara?" she said to the Twins. "'Tis nowhere else at all now but on the flag, but time was, long, long years ago, when the harp itself was played on Tara's hill. And in those days there were poets to praise Ireland, and singers to sing her songs. And here they will be telling of those days, and singing those songs. Come and listen. 'Tis a Feis (pronounced faysh) they're having, and prizes given for the best tale told, or the best song sung."

The old woman and the Twins made their way to the platform and sat down on a bench near the edge of it. Many other people were sitting or standing about. An old man stood up on the platform. He told the story of Cuchulain (pronounced Koohoolin)—the "Hound of Culain"—and how he fought all the greatest warriors of the world on the day he first took arms.

When he had finished, another man took his place and told the story of Deirdre and Naisi, and another told the fate of the four children of Lir that were turned into four beautiful swans by their cruel stepmother.

And when the stories were finished a prize was given for the best one, and the Twins were glad that it was for the story of Deirdre, for that tale was like an old friend to them.

After that there was music, and the dances of old Ireland— the reel and the lilt. And when last of all came the Irish jig, the old woman put her basket down on the ground.

"Sure, the music is like the springtime in my bones," she said to the Twins. "Be-dad, I'd the foot of the world on me when I was a girl and I can still shake one with the best of them, if I do say it myself."

She put her hands on her hips and began to dance! The music got into everybody else's bones, too, and soon everybody around the platform, and on it, too,—old and young, large and small,—was dancing gayly to the sound of it.

The Twins danced with the rest, and they were having such a good time that they might have forgotten to go home at all if all of a sudden, Larry hadn't shaken Eileen's arm and said, "Look there!"

"Where?" Eileen said. "There!" said Larry. "The rough man with the brown horse."

The moment Eileen saw the man with the brown horse she took Larry's hand and they both ran as fast as they could back to their Father.

"We saw the Tinker!" they cried the moment they saw Mr McQueen.

"Then we'd as well be starting home," said Mr McQueen. "I'd rather not be meeting the gentleman on the road after dark." He got Colleen and put her into the cart once more. Then he and the Twins had something to eat. They bought a ginger cake shaped like a rabbit, and another like a man from one of the hawkers, and they bought some sugar-sticks, too, and these, with what they had brought from home, made their supper.

Then Mr McQueen brought out his notched stick. "We've sold the pig," he said, with his finger on the first notch, "and the butter and eggs was the second notch." Then he went over all the other notches. "And besides all else I've bought Herself a shawl," he said to the Twins.

The Twins wanted to get home because the Secret was getting so big inside of them, they knew they couldn't possibly hold it in much longer, and they didn't want to let it out until they were at home and could tell their Father and Mother both at the same time. So they said good-bye to Diddy, and Eileen took off the ribbons and kept them to remember her by. Then they hurried away.

It was after dark when at last they drove into the yard. Mrs McQueen came running to the door to greet them and hear all about the Fair.

Eileen and Larry told her about the prize, and about Lady Kathleen buying the pig, and about seeing the Tinker, while their Father was putting up Colleen.

Then when he came in with all his bundles, and took the three golden sovereigns out of his pocket, to show to the Mother, the Twins couldn't keep still another minute. "It's for you! To pay the rent!" they cried.

The Father and Mother looked at each other. "Now, what are they at all," said Mrs McQueen, "but the best children in the width of the world? Wasn't I after telling you that we'd make it out somehow? And to think of her being a thoroughbred like that, and we never knowing it at all." She meant the pig!

But Mr McQueen never said a word. He just gave Larry and Eileen a great hug. Then Mr McQueen went over all the errands with his wife, and last of all he brought out the shawl. "There, old woman," he said, "is a fairing for you!"

"The Saints be praised for this day!" cried Mrs McQueen. "The rent paid, and me with a fine new shawl the equal of any in the parish."

It was a happy family that went to bed in the little farmhouse that night. Only Mrs McQueen didn't sleep well. She got up a number of times in the night to be sure there were no Tinkers prowling about. "For one can't be too careful with so much money in the house," she said to herself.

Chapter Fourteen.

Sunday.

The next Sunday all the McQueen family went to Mass and
Mrs McQueen wore her new shawl. The chapel was quite a
distance away, and as they walked and all the neighbours
walked, too, they had a pleasant time talking together along
the way.

Dennis and the Twins walked together, and Larry and
Eileen told Dennis all about the Fair, and about selling the
pig to the Lady Kathleen, and "Begorra," said Dennis, "but
that little pig was after bringing you all the luck in the
world, wasn't she?" All the other boys and girls wanted to
hear about it. Most of them had never been to a Fair. So
Eileen and Larry talked all the way to church, and that was
two miles and a half of talk, the shortest way you could go.

Just as they neared the church, what should they see but
Grannie Malone, coming in grandeur, riding on a jaunting-
car! Beside her was a big man with a tall hat on his head.

"'Tis her son Michael, back from the States!" cried the
Twins. "He said in a letter he was coming."

They ran as fast as they could to reach the church door in
time to see them go in. Everybody else stopped, too, they
were so surprised, and everybody said to everybody else,
"Well, for dear's sake, if that's not Michael Malone come
back to see his old Mother!"

And then they whispered among themselves, "Look at the
grand clothes on him, and the scarf pin the bigness of a

ha'penny piece, and the hat! Sure, America must be the rich place entirely."

And when Michael got out of the cart and helped out his old Mother, there were many hands held out for him to shake, and many old neighbours for him to greet.

"This is a proud day for you, Grannie Malone," said Mrs McQueen.

"It is," said Grannie, "and a sad day, too, for he's after taking me back to America, and 'tis likely I'll never set my two eyes on old Ireland again, when once the width of the sea comes between us."

She wiped her eyes as she spoke. Then the bell rang to call the people into the chapel. It was little the congregation heard of the service that day, for however much they tried they couldn't help looking at the back of Michael's head and at Grannie's bonnet.

And afterward, when all the people were outside the church door, Grannie Malone said to different old friends of Michael, "Come along to my house this afternoon, and listen to Himself telling about the States!"

That afternoon when the McQueens had finished their noon meal, the whole family walked up the road to Grannie's house. There were a good many people there before them. Grannie's little house was full to the door. Michael stood by the fireplace, and as the McQueens came in he was saying, "It's the truth I'm telling you! There are over forty States in the Union, and many of them bigger than the whole of Ireland itself! There are places in it where you could travel as far as from Dublin to Belfast without ever seeing a town at all; just fields without stones or trees lying there begging for the plough, and sorrow a person to give it them!"

"Will you listen to that now?" said Grannie.

"And more than that, if you'll believe me," Michael went on, "there do be places in America where they give away land, let alone buying it! Just by going and living on it for a time and doing a little work on it, you can get one hundred and sixty acres of land, for your own, mind you!"

"The Saints preserve us, but that might be like Heaven itself, if I may make bold to say so," said Mrs Maguire.

"You may well say that, Mrs Maguire," Michael answered, "for there, when a man has bent his back, and put in sweat and labour to enrich the land, it is not for some one else he does it, but for himself and his children. Of course, the land that is given away is far from big cities, and it's queer and lonely sometimes on the distant farms, for they do not live in villages, as we do, but each farmhouse is by itself on its own land, and no neighbours handy. So for myself, I stayed in the big city."

"You seem to have prospered, Michael," said Mr McQueen.

"I have so," Michael answered. "There are jobs in plenty for the willing hands. Sure, no Irishman would give up at all when there's always something new to try. And there's always somebody from the old sod there to help you if the luck turns on you. Do you remember Patrick Doran, now? He lived forninst the blacksmith shop years ago. Well, Patrick is a great man. He's a man of fortune, and a good friend to myself. One year when times were hard, and work not so plenty, I lost my job, and didn't Patrick help me to another the very next week? Not long after that Patrick ran for Alderman, and myself and many another like me, worked hard for to get him elected, and since then I've been in politics myself. First Patrick got me a job on the police force, and then I was Captain, and since then, by one change and another, if I do say it, I'm an Alderman myself!"

"It's wonderful, sure," Mr Maguire said, when Michael had finished, "but I'm not wishful for to change. Sure, old Ireland is good enough for me, and I'd not be missing the larks singing in the spring in the green fields of Erin, and the smell of the peat on the hearth in winter. It's queer and lonesome I'd be without these things, and that's the truth."

He threw his head back and began to sing. Everybody joined in and sang, too. This is the song they sang:—

"Old Ireland you're my jewel sure,

My heart's delight and glory,

Till Time shall pass his empty glass

Your name shall live in story.

"And this shall be the song for me,

The first my heart was learning,

When first my tongue its accents flung,

Old Ireland, you're my darling!

"From Dublin Bay to Cork's Sweet Cove,

Old Ireland, you're my darling

My darling, my darling,

From Dublin Bay to Cork's Sweet Cove;

Old Ireland, you're my darling."

Chapter Fifteen.

Mr McQueen makes up his Mind.

Michael sang with the others. And when the song was
ended, he said, "'Tis a true word, Mr Maguire, that there's
no place like old Ireland; and you'll not find an Irishman
anywhere in America that wouldn't put the man down that
said a word against her. But what with the landlords taking
every shilling you can scrape together and charging you
higher rent whenever you make a bit of an improvement on
your farm, there's no chance at all to get on in the world.
And with the children, God bless them, coming along by
sixes and dozens, and little for them to do at home, and no
place to put them when they grow up, sure, it's well to go
where they've a better chance.

"Look at the schools now! If you could see the school that
my Patrick goes to, you'd never rest at all until your
children had the same! Sure, the schoolhouses are like
palaces over there, and as for learning, the children pick it
up as a hen does corn!"

"And are there no faults with America, whatever?" Mr
McQueen said to Michael.

"There do be faults with her," Michael answered, "and I'll
never be the man to say otherwise. There's plenty of things
to be said about America that would leave you thinking 'tis
a long way this side of Heaven. But whatever it is that's
wrong, 'tis the people themselves that make it so, and by
the same token it is themselves that can cure the trouble
when they're so minded. It's not like having your troubles
put down on you by the people that's above you, and that

you can't reach at all for to be correcting them! All I say is there's a better chance over there for yourself and the children."

The Twins and Dennis and the other young people were getting tired of sitting still by this time, and when Michael stopped talking about America they jumped up. The children ran outdoors and played tag around Grannie's house, and the older people stayed inside.

By and by Grannie came to the door and called them. "Come in, every one of you," she cried, "and have a fine bit of cake with currants in it! Sure, Michael brought the currants and all the things for to make it yesterday, thinking maybe there'd be neighbours in. And maybe 'tis the last bit of cake I'll be making for you at all, for 'tis but two weeks now until we start across the water." She wiped her eyes on her apron.

Mr McQueen was very quiet as he walked home with Mrs McQueen and the Twins. And that evening, after the children were in bed, he sat for a long time silent, with his pipe in his mouth. His pipe went out and he did not notice it. By and by he said to Mrs McQueen, "I've made up my mind—"

"The Lord save us! To what?" said Mrs McQueen.

"To go to America," said Mr McQueen.

Mrs McQueen hid her face in her hands and rocked back and forth and cried. "To be leaving the place I was born, and where my father and mother were born before me, and all the neighbours, and this old house that's been home since ever I married you—'twill break the heart in my body," she said.

"I like that part of it no better than yourself," said Mr McQueen, "but when I think of the years to come, and Larry and Eileen growing up to work as hard as we have worked without getting much at all, and think of the better chance altogether they'll have over there, sure, I can't be thinking of the pain, but only of the hope there is in it for them."

"I've seen this coming ever since the children told us about Grannie Malone's letter," said Mrs McQueen. "'Tis Michael has put this in your head."

"'Tis not Michael alone," said Mr McQueen; "'tis also other things. To-morrow I pay Conroy the rent money. And it will take all that the pig brought and all I've been able to rake and scrape myself, and nothing left over at all. And there's but ourselves and the Twins, and the year has not been a bad one. We have had the pig, which we wouldn't be having another year. And what would it be like if there were more of us to feed, and no more pigs to be found in the bog like manna from Heaven, to be helping us out?"

"Sure, if it's for the children," sobbed Mrs McQueen, "I'd go anywhere in the world, and that you know well."

"I do know it," said Mr McQueen. "And since we're going at all, let it be soon. We'll go with Grannie and Michael."

"In two weeks' time?" cried Mrs McQueen.

"We will so," said Mr McQueen. "I've no debts behind me, and we can sell the cows and hens, and take with us whatever we need from the house. Michael Malone will lend me the money and find me a job when we get there. The likes of this chance will never befall us again, and faith, we'll take it."

"Did he tell you so?" asked Mrs McQueen.

"He did, indeed."

"Well, then, I've no other word to say, and if it must be done, the sooner the better," said Mrs McQueen.

That night she lay awake a long time. She was planning just what they should take with them to their new home, and trying to think what the new home would be like.

Chapter Sixteen.

Mr McQueen pays the Rent.

The next morning Mr McQueen went to Mr Conroy and paid the rent. Then he said, "This is the last rent I'll be paying you, Mr Conroy!"

Mr Conroy was surprised. "What do you mean by that?" he said.

"I mean that I'm going to leave old Ireland," said Mr McQueen.

"Well, now!" cried Mr Conroy. "To think of a sensible man like yourself leaving a good farm to go off, dear knows where! And you not knowing what you'll do when you get there as like as any way! I thought you had better sense, McQueen."

"It's because of my better sense that I'm going," said Mr McQueen. "Faith, do you think I'd be showing the judgment of an old goat to stay where every penny I can get out of the land I have to pay back in rent? I'm going to America where there'll be a chance for myself."

"I thought Michael Malone would be sowing the seeds of discontent in this parish, with his silk hats and his grand talk," said Mr Conroy angrily, "but I didn't think you were the fish to be caught with fine words!"

"If the seeds of discontent have been sown in this parish, Terence Conroy," said Mr McQueen, "'tis you and the likes of you that have ploughed and harrowed the ground ready for them! Do you think we're wishful to be leaving our old homes and all our friends? But 'tis you that makes it too hard entirely for people to stay. And I can tell you that if you keep on with others as you have with me, raising the rent when any work is done to improve the farm, you'll be left in time with no tenants at all. And then where will you be yourself, Terence Conroy?"

Mr Conroy's face was red with anger, but he said, "While I'm not needing you to teach me my duty, I will say this, McQueen. You're a good farmer, and I hate to see you do a foolish thing for yourself. If you'll stay on the farm, I'll not raise the rent on you."

"You're too late, altogether," said Mr McQueen; "and as you said yourself I'm not the fish to be caught with fine words. I know better than to believe you. I'll be sailing from Queenstown in two weeks' time."

And with that he stalked out of the room and slammed the door, leaving Mr Conroy in a very bad state of mind.

All that Larry and Eileen could remember of the next two weeks was a queer jumble of tears and good-byes, of good wishes and blessings, and strange, strange feelings they had never had before. Their Mother went about with a white face and red eyes, and their Father was very silent as he packed the few household belongings they were to take with them to their new home.

At last the great day came. The McQueens got up very early that morning, ate their potatoes and drank their tea from a few cracked and broken dishes which were to be left behind. Then, when they had tidied up the hearth and put on their wraps ready to go, Mrs McQueen brought some water to quench the fire on the hearth. She might almost have quenched it with her tears. And as she poured the water upon the ashes she crooned this little song (see Note 1) sadly to herself:—

"Vein of my heart, from the lone mountain

The smoke of the turf will die.

And the stream that sang to the young children

Run down alone from the sky—

On the doorstone, grass - and the

Cloud lying

Where they lie

In the old country."

Mr McQueen and the Twins stood still with their bundles in their hands until she had finished and risen from her knees, then they went quietly out the door, all four together, and closed it after them.

Mrs McQueen stooped to gather a little bunch of shamrock leaves which grew by the doorstone, and then the McQueen family was quite, quite ready for the long journey.

Mr Maguire had bought Colleen and the cows, and he was to have the few hens that were left for taking the McQueen family to the train.

Larry and Eileen saw him coming up the road, "Here comes Mr Maguire with the cart!" they cried, "and Dennis is driving the jaunting-car with Michael and Grannie on it."

They soon reached the little group by the roadside, and then the luggage was loaded into the cart. Mrs McQueen got up with Grannie on one side of the jaunting-car and Eileen sat between them. Michael and Mr McQueen were on the other side with Larry. The small bags and bundles were put in the well of the jaunting-car.

"Get up!" cried Dennis, and off they started. Mrs McQueen looked back at the old house, and cried into her new shawl. Grannie was crying, too. But Michael said, "Wait until you see your new home, and sure, you'll be crying to think you weren't in it before!" And that cheered them up again, and soon a turn in the road hid the old house from their sight forever.

The luggage was heavy, and Colleen was slow. So it took several hours to reach the railroad. It took longer, too, because all the people in the village ran out of their houses to say good-bye. When they passed the schoolhouse, the Master gave the children leave to say good-bye to the Twins. He even came out to the road himself and shook hands with everybody.

But for all that, when the train came rattling into the station, there they all were on the platform in a row ready to get on board. When it stopped, the guard jumped down and opened the door of a compartment. He put Grannie in first, then Mrs McQueen and the Twins. They were dreadfully afraid the train would start before Mr McQueen and Michael and all the luggage were on board.

It was the first time Grannie had ever seen a train, or the Twins either. But at last they were all in, and the guard locked the door. Larry and Eileen looked out of the window and waved their hands to Mr Maguire and Dennis. The engine whistled, the wheels began to turn, and above the noise the Twins heard Dennis call out to them, "Sure, I'll be coming along to America myself some day."

"We'll be watching for you," Eileen called back.

Then they passed the station, and were soon racing along over the open fields at what seemed to poor Grannie a fearful rate of speed.

"Murder! murder!" she screamed. "Is it for this I left my cabin? To be broken in bits on the track like a piece of old crockery! Wirra, wirra, why did I ever let myself be persuaded at all? Ochanee, but it is Himself has the soothering tongue in his mouth to coax his old Mother away for to destroy her entirely!"

Michael laughed and patted her arm, and "Whist now," he said, "sure, I'd never bring you where harm would come to you, and that you know well. Look out of the window, for 'tis the last you'll be seeing of old Ireland."

Grannie dried her eyes, but still she clung to Michael's arm, and when the train went around a curve she crossed herself and told her beads as fast as she could.

The Twins were not frightened. They were busy seeing things. And besides, Larry had Grannie's piece of coal in his pocket. From the window they caught glimpses of distant blue hills, and of lakes still more blue. They passed by many a brown bog, and many a green field with farmers and farmers' wives working in them. The hillsides were blue with blossoming flax, and once they passed a field all spread with white linen bleaching in the sun.

They flew by little towns with queer names, like Ballygrady and Ballylough, and once when they were quite near Cork they saw the towers of Blarney Castle.

At last the train rattled into a great station. There was so much noise from puffing engines and rumbling trucks and shouting men, that the Twins could only take hold of their Mother's hands and keep close behind their Father as he followed Michael, with Grannie clinging to him, to another train. Then there were more flying fields, and a city and more fields still, until they reached Queenstown.

The next thing they knew they were walking across a gangplank and on to a boat. The Twins had never seen anything larger than a rowboat before, and this one looked very big to them, though it was only a lighter. This lighter was to carry luggage and passengers from the dock to the great steamer lying outside the harbour in the deep water of the main channel.

When they were all safely on board the lighter, and Michael had counted their bundles to be sure they had not lost anything, the Twins and their Father and Mother, with Michael and Grannie, stood by the deck rail and looked back at the dock. It was crowded with people running to and fro. There were groups of other emigrants like themselves, surrounded by great piles of luggage—waiting for the next lighter, for one boat would not carry all who wanted to go.

There were many good-byes being said and many tears falling, and in the midst of all the noise and confusion the sailors were loading tons of barrels and bags and boxes and trunks on board the ship.

There was no friend to see them off, but when they saw people crying all about them, the Twins cried a little, too, for sympathy, and even Mr McQueen's eyes were red along the rims.

At last the gangplanks were drawn in, and the cables thrown off. The screws began to churn the green water into white foam, and the boat moved slowly out of the harbour.

The Twins and their Father and Mother, with Grannie and Michael, stood by the rail for a long time, and watched the crowd on the pier until it grew smaller and smaller, and at last disappeared entirely from sight around a bend in the Channel.

They stood there until the lighter reached the great ship that was waiting to take them across the water to a new world.

And when at last they were safely on board, and the lighters had gone back empty into the harbour, they stood on the wide deck of the ship, with their faces turned toward Ireland, until all they could see of it in the gathering dusk was a strip of dark blue against the eastern sky, with little lights in cottage windows twinkling from it like tiny stars.

Then they turned their faces toward the bright western sky.

Note 1. Copyright of this poem by Herbert Trench, held by John Lane.

Chapter Seventeen.

Twenty Years After.

In the middle of one of the busiest crossings in Chicago, there stands a big man in a blue uniform. His eyes are blue, and there are wrinkles in the corners of them, the marks of many smiles.

On his head is a blue cap, and under the edge of the cap you catch a glimpse of dark hair. There are bands of gold braid on his sleeve, and on his breast is a large silver star.

He is King of the Crossing. When he blows his whistle, all the street-cars and automobiles and carriages—even if it were the carriage of the Mayor himself—stop stock-still. Then he waves his white-gloved hands and the stream of people pours across the street.

If there is a very small boy among them, the King of the Crossing sometimes lays a big hand on his shoulder and goes with him to the curb. And he has been known to carry a small girl across on his shoulder and set her safely down on the other side.

When the people are all across, he goes back to the middle of the street once more, and blows twice on his little whistle.

Then all the wheels that have been standing as still as if they had gone to sleep suddenly wake up, and go rolling down the street, while those that have just been turning stop and wait while the big man helps more people over the crossing the other way.

All day long the King of the Crossing stands there, blowing his whistle, waving his white-gloved hands, and turning the stream of people up first one street, then the other.

Everybody minds him. If everybody didn't, they might get run over and wake up in a hospital. Oh, he must be minded, the King of the Crossing, or nobody would be safe!

When the long day is over, he looks up the street and sees another big man coming. This man wears a blue uniform, too, and a silver star, and when the hands on the big clock at the corner point to five, he steps into the place of the King of the Crossing and reigns in his stead.

Then the King jumps on to the platform of a passing street-car, and by and by, when it has gone several miles, he jumps off again, and walks up the street to a little house that's as neat as neat can be.

It stands back from the street in a little green yard. The house is painted white, and the front door is green. But he doesn't go to the front door. He goes round by the sidewalk to the kitchen door, and there he doesn't even knock.

He opens the door and walks right in. Through the open door comes the smell of something good cooking, and he sees a plump woman with blue eyes that have smile wrinkles in the corners, just like his own, and crinkly dark hair, just like his own, too, bending over the stove. She is just tasting the something that smells so good, with a spoon.

When she sees the big man in the door she tastes so quickly that she burns her tongue! But she can use it just the same even if it is burned.

She runs to the big man and says, "And is that yourself, now, Larry darling? Sure, I'm that glad to see you, I've scalded myself with the soup!"

The big man has just time to say, "Sure, Eileen, you were always a great one for burning yourself. Do you remember that day at Grannie Malone's"—when out into the kitchen tumble a little Larry and a little Eileen, and a Baby. They have heard his voice, and they fall upon the King of the Crossing as if he weren't a King at all—but just a plain ordinary Uncle.

They take off his cap and rumple his hair. They get into his pockets and find some peppermints there. And the Baby even tries to get the silver star off his breast to put into her mouth.

"Look at that now," cries Uncle Larry. "Get along with you! Is it trying to take me off the Force, you are? Sure, that star was never intended by the City for you to cut your teeth on."

"She'll poison herself with the things she's always after putting in her mouth," cries the Mother. She seizes the Baby and sets her in a safe corner by herself, gives her a spoon and says, "There now—you can be cutting your teeth on that."

And when the children have quite worn Uncle Larry out, he sits upon the floor, where they have him by this time, and runs his fingers through his hair, which is standing straight up, and says to the Mother, "Sure, Eileen, when you and I were children on the old sod, we were never such spalpeens as the likes of these! They have me destroyed entirely, and me the biggest policeman on the Force! Is it American they are, or Irish, I want to know?"

"It's Irish-American we are," shouts little Larry.

"And with the heft of both countries in your fists," groans big Larry.

And then the Mother, who has been laying the table, meanwhile, interferes. "Come off of your poor Uncle," she says, "and be eating your soup, like gentlemen and ladies. It's getting cold on you waiting for you to finish your antics. Your poor Uncle Larry won't come near you at all, and you all the time punishing him like that."

And then the Baby, still sucking her spoon, is lifted into her high chair. A chair is placed for Uncle Larry, and they all eat their soup around the kitchen table, just as the very last rays of the summer sun make long streaks of light across the kitchen floor.

"Where's Dennis?" says Uncle Larry, while the children are quiet for a moment.

"Oh, it's Himself is so late that I feed the children and put them to bed before he gets home at all," says the Mother. "It's little he sees of them except of a Sunday."

"It's likely he'll live the longer for that," says Uncle Larry. He looks reproachfully at the children and rubs his head.

And then—"Mother, tell us, what kind of a boy was Uncle Larry when you and he were Twins and lived in Ireland," says little Eileen.

"The best in the width of the world," says her Mother promptly. "Weren't you, Larry? Speak up and tell them now."

And Uncle Larry laughs and says, "Sure, I was too good entirely! It wouldn't be modest to tell you the truth about myself."

"Tell us about Mother, then," says little Eileen. "Was she the best in the width of the world, too?"

"Sure, I'll never be telling tales on my only twin sister," says Uncle Larry, "beyond telling you that there was many another in green old Ireland just like her, whatever kind she was. But I can't stay here wearing out my tongue! Look out the window! The chickens have gone to roost, and the sun is down. So get along with you to your beds."

When he had gone, and the children were in bed, and the house quiet, the Mother sat down by the light in the kitchen with a basket of mending beside her.

And while she darned and mended and waited for Himself to come home, she remembered and remembered about when she was little Eileen, herself, and the King of the Crossing was just her twin brother Larry.

And this book is what she remembered.

Appendix.

Suggestions to Teachers.

Like the author's earlier books—"The Dutch Twins" and "The Japanese Twins"—this reader aims to foster a kindly feeling and a deserved respect for a country whose children have come to form a numerous portion of our own population.

During the reading, point out Ireland on a map of the world or on a globe, and tell the children something about the unique character of the country, thus connecting this supplementary reading material with the work in geography.

The text is so simply written that any fourth or fifth grade child can read it without much preparation. In the fourth grade it may be well to have the children read it first in a study period in order to work out the pronunciation of the more difficult words. In the fifth grade the children can usually read it at sight, without the preparatory study. Give little attention to the expressions in dialect. Let the children read them naturally and they will enhance the dramatic effect of the story. The possibilities in the story for dramatisation and for language and constructive work will be immediately apparent.

In connection with the reading of the book, teachers should read or tell to the children stories of Irish life and from Irish folk-lore; for example, "The Story of the Little Rid Hin," "The Dagda's Harp," and "The Tailor and the Three Beasts," in Sara Cone Bryant's Stories to Tell to Children;

and "Billy Beg and his Bull," in the same author's How to Tell Stories to Children. Material which may readily be adapted to this use will be found in Johnston and Spencer's Ireland's Story. Let the children bring to class postcards and other pictures of scenes in Ireland.

These are only a few of the many ways that will occur to resourceful teachers for making the book a valuable as well as an enjoyable exercise in reading.

Made in the USA
Coppell, TX
29 November 2021

66672978R00056